RUSTY'S TRAIN RIDE

Heather Amery
Illustrated by Stephen Cartwright

Edited by Jenny Tyler
Language Consultant: Betty Root

There is a little yellow duck to find on every page.

This is Apple Tree Farm.

This is Mrs. Boot, the farmer. She has two children, called Poppy and Sam, and a dog called Rusty.

They are having breakfast.

"What are we doing today?" says Sam. "Let's go and see the old steam train," says Mrs. Boot.

"Come on, Rusty," says Sam.

They walk down the road to the station. "Don't let Rusty go. Hold him tight," says Mrs. Boot.

They wait on the platform.

Mrs. Boot, Poppy and Sam watch the train come in. Mrs. Hill and her puppy watch with them.

The train is ready to go.

Everyone talks to the train driver. The fireman shuts the doors. He climbs on the train.

"Where's my puppy?"

"Mopp was with me on the platform," says Mrs. Hill. "Now he's gone." The train starts to move.

Rusty watches it go.

He pulls and pulls and runs away. Then he
jumps through an open carriage window.

"Come back, Rusty," shouts Sam.

Rusty looks out of the window. "There he is," says Poppy. "He's going for a train ride on his own."

"Stop, stop the train," shouts Sam.

Mrs. Boot, Poppy and Sam shout and wave.
But the train puffs away down the track.

"What shall we do?"

"Both dogs have gone," says Sam. "We'll have to wait for the train to come back," says Mrs. Boot.

At last, the train comes back.

"Look, there's Rusty," says Sam. "You naughty dog, where have you been?" says Poppy.

The train stops at the station.

The fireman climbs down from the engine. He opens the carriage door.

"Come on, Rusty."

"Your ride on the train is over," says Mrs. Boot.
Rusty jumps down. "What's he got?" says Sam.

"It's my little Mopp."

Mrs. Hill picks up her puppy. "Poor little thing.
Did you go on the train all by yourself?"

"Rusty went with him," says Sam.

"That's why he jumped on the train," says Poppy.
"Clever Rusty," says Sam.

First published in 1999 by Usborne Publishing Ltd., Usborne House, 83-85 Saffron Hill, London EC1N 8RT, England. www.usborne.com
Copyright © 1999 Usborne Publishing Ltd.